JIMMY
AND THE
BANSHEE

DAN KISSANE

Illustrated by Celine Kiernan

THE O'BRIEN PRESS
DUBLIN

First published 1999 by The O'Brien Press Ltd,
20 Victoria Road, Dublin 6, Ireland.
Tel: +353 1 4923333; Fax: +353 1 4922777
E-mail: books@obrien.ie
Website: www.obrien.ie
Reprinted 2000, 2003.

ISBN: 0-86278-549-9

British Library Cataloguing-in-Publication Data
Kissane, Dan
Jimmy and the banshee
1.Children's stories
I.Title
823.9'14[J]

3 4 5 6 7 8 9
03 04 05 06 07 08

Editing, typesetting, layout and design: The O'Brien Press Ltd
Illustrations: Celine Kiernan
Printing: Cox & Wyman Ltd

CONTENTS

Post Nubila Phoebus

Acknowledgements

I would like to thank Rachel Pierce, Eilis French,
Lynn Pierce, the illustrators and all the staff
at The O'Brien Press.

WELL!

'JAMES McELHATTON!' My name rang around the classroom. Most people don't mind the sound of their own names, but I have to say that I never really cared for mine. That's the name I was christened with, right enough, but nobody ever called me by it except Mr O'Shea, the schoolmaster. The McElhatton part wasn't too bad, but when he put the James before it, I knew I was in trouble.

That particular day was a Friday, if I remember right, and it was during our afternoon lesson that my name was called. Mr O'Shea had picked on Mikey McGrory, my best friend, and asked him to give the Irish word for a 'well'. Now, *my* Irish was fairly good, because I had learned at home with my grandfather, but poor Mikey! There is more hair on the shell of a new-laid egg than there was Irish on Mikey McGrory's tongue.

He had one of those faces that looks as though

someone has sat on it, and with his red hair standing up in spikes, he looked like he had been dragged backwards through a hedge. He just sat there, staring into space, saying nothing. You couldn't help feeling sorry for him.

Mr O'Shea stared back at him. Have you ever seen the way a frog stares at a fly before he flicks out his tongue to eat him? Well, that's the way Mr O'Shea stared at Mikey McGrory.

My desk was next to Mikey's and, in desperation, he shot a glance across at me – one of those -*besieging* or *beseeching* glances. I'm not sure which is right, because those big words always mix me up, but it was one of those glances that say: '*Help*!'

Anyway, I couldn't very well let him down. I put my hand up to my mouth and hissed across at him, '*Tobar*!' And it was at that moment that my name echoed around the classroom. 'JAMES McELHATTON!'

I looked up, trying to seem as innocent as possible. 'Yes, sir?'

'*Yes, sir*!' Mr O'Shea repeated. 'Since when, James McElhatton, have you been the instructor of this class?'

I said nothing. It was no good trying to fence words with Mr O'Shea, his tongue was much too sharp.

The upshot of it was that, when school was finished for the day, he kept me in and made me write on the blackboard one hundred times: 'I will not disrupt the lesson.' *A hundred times*! Can you imagine? And I didn't even know what the word 'disrupt' *meant*!

After a long time I got it all done. Four columns of writing, with twenty-five lines in each column. By this time, I was so sick of it that I made up my mind that if I ever found out what 'disrupt' meant, I would do it to the class first chance I got.

When I'd finished, Mikey was waiting for me outside in the yard – which was the least he could do, seeing as it was because of him I got into trouble in the first place. He was sitting on the wall, sucking a penny lolly.

I was feeling pretty fed up, but Mikey soon cheered me up – that's the kind of fellow he was. 'Himself and his wells!' he snorted. 'Pity someone wouldn't get him and put him digging one in a stony place, and then, when he had it dug, make him stand in the bottom and fill it in on top of him!' The thought of that put a smile on my face, and we wandered away from the school.

'Speaking of wells,' Mikey said after a bit, jumping off the wall and crunching up the last of his lolly, 'let's go and take a look at the old wishing-well down at Hegarty's place. I haven't been there for ages.' That seemed like a good idea, and the two of us struck off down the road.

It was early June, and the afternoon sun was hot. Haymaking was in full swing, and the air everywhere was charged with the lovely smells of the season. Now and then, as we walked along, we saw gangs of men working in the meadows near the road. Some of them were tossing up the newly mown grass for the sun and breeze to get through, while others were further ahead with their crop and were drawing it together and making it up into haycocks. By rights, Mikey and myself should have been in some field or other, helping out, but we had been at that for the last four evenings and we were sick of it.

Anyway, we were soon out of sight of the haymakers, because we turned off the road and made our way down the old laneway which led to Hegarty's place. Along each side, the untended whitethorn hedges had grown tall and spindly, and they were full of twittering greenfinches which took flight as we passed. Eventually, we came to an old, abandoned farmyard. It was surrounded by thick, high hedges of holly and laurel, which in places had completely closed in at the top, so that the place had a mysterious sort of feel to it, like an empty church.

The house that had once stood in the centre of the yard had long since fallen down. There was no sign of the roof left, and a lot of the stone walling had collapsed in on itself. It must have been a hundred years or more since Miss Hegarty – whoever she was – had lived there. Even my grandfather, who was the oldest man in the village, couldn't remember her. He only knew a few half-remembered stories which he had heard in his youth. The gist of those was that Miss Hegarty had been some kind of a fairy-woman or a witch or something, but it was all very vague, and no one really knew anything for certain.

Around the back of the old house, there was a well. It was walled in on three sides with stone flags which had been set into the ground. In front, there was a smooth, flat, black rock, and the water from the well trickled steadily over it and flowed away in a narrow stream. On that rock a sign had been carved. It looked like this:

$$\delta$$

No one knew what the mark was, or what it meant, but there was definitely something strange about it; you could just *feel* that when you looked at it. Over the years, people had come from miles around to throw coins into that well and make wishes there. The water was ice-cold and as clear as crystal, and deep down in the bottom you could see layers of coins: pennies, ha'pennies, threepenny bits and even the odd sixpence and shilling.

Nobody ever tried to take any of them out, because it was well known that a man had attempted it once, years ago, and as he did, a hand had shot out from the water, grabbed him, and pulled him down into the well! Down, down, down, he went, and never seen again.

That might only have been a legend, of course, but ask yourself: would you take the chance for the sake of a few handfuls of pennies?

Mikey stared doubtfully into the well. 'Last time I was here,' he said, 'I threw in a penny and wished for an aeroplane.'

'What happened?' I asked.

'Well, I didn't get an aeroplane – that's for sure. But that same night a bat got into my room and spent the night flying around. I expect that was the best the well could manage at such short notice.'

'It wasn't so far out, either,' I agreed. 'They both have wings.'

Mikey began rummaging in his pockets. After a bit he drew out a penny and looked at it. 'I'll give it another chance!' he declared, and, crossing his fingers, he flipped the penny into the water.

I had never had much luck with wishes myself, by means of wishing-wells or any other way, but seeing as I had come that far, I decided to give it a go. All I had about me was a threepenny bit, and that was all the money I had in the world. I know threepence doesn't seem like much now, but in those days it was worth quite a bit.

It took me a while to make my mind up, but I did in the end. If the wish came true, I said to myself, it would be worth it. I crossed my fingers as Mikey had done and, with a flick of my thumb, I sent my little coin spinning through the air. It landed with a splash in the well.

Mikey stared at me in amazement. 'Three-pence!' he gasped. 'Must be some wish!'

I nodded. It was.

2

A DEVIL'S COACH-HORSE

I know you're not supposed to tell a wish, because if you do, it won't come true. But seeing as all this happened long ago, I don't suppose there's any harm in letting you know now what it was I wished for with my threepenny bit.

Over the fields, about a mile away from our house, the McCafferty family lived. Nobody in our village was what you would call rich, but the McCaffertys were a bit poorer than most. They had only one cow, and she was a bony old screw that hardly gave them enough milk to colour their tea. The few pigs they had weren't much to look at either – I heard my grandfather say once that they used to tie knots in their tails to stop them going out through the crack in the door of the sty, but I think that wasn't very likely. They had a few hens, too, but they were nothing to write home about – the heaviest part of them was their feathers. And as a result of all that, there was never too much food on the McCaffertys' table. It was tough for them, because Mr and Mrs McCafferty worked just as hard as anyone else in the village. It was just that they had more expenses than most people because of their daughter, Katie.

Katie was in the same class as me at school. At least, she was most of the time, but she used to be missing a lot, because she was often sick and stayed at home. When that happened, she would fall behind in her lessons, but she always caught up easily when she came back, and even found time to help me with my arithmetic. I always found that subject kind of tough, though I was quick enough at the rest of them – except for that old history and some of that geography and, like I said, those big words in English. But anyway, Katie always found time for me when she was well enough.

But she wasn't well now, she was sick, and had been for a long while. I don't know what exactly was wrong with her, but it was something serious. Dr O'Halloran used to visit her two or three times a week, and the medicine she had to take used up nearly all the money her parents were able to earn.

Sometimes my mother used to send me over to their house with a parcel of eggs or a piece of bacon for the pot, but I always had to watch for my chance when Mr McCafferty was away, because he was a very proud man. On those visits, I used to sit by Katie's bed for a while and talk to her. In spite of her illness, she was always happy and smiling, and she would ask me to tell her all about what went on at school and so on.

Between you and me, I was very fond of Katie. She wasn't exactly what you would call pretty, because her nose was a bit turned-up and freckly, and her mouth was a bit lopsided; but I liked her. And what I am trying to say is that that's where my threepence went: I wished for Katie McCafferty to get better.

After I had parted from Mikey, I hurried home. I didn't like to be too late, because there were always a few jobs waiting for me. There were hens to feed, and pigsties to be cleaned out, and maybe a row of cabbages to be weeded. But I didn't get to do any of those jobs that evening, because just as I got home, whose car should I see pulling out of the yard but Dr O'Halloran's.

That gave me a bit of a fright, and I ran into the house. 'Is anything wrong?' I asked, staring around me. 'I saw the doctor's car.'

'There's nothing wrong,' said my mother, turning from the table where she was making bread. 'Doctor O'Halloran was around visiting young Katie McCafferty, and while he was in the neighbourhood, he called to see Grandfather.'

'What's wrong with him?' I asked anxiously.

'Nothing at all, only the doctor says he has to give up smoking his pipe.'

Grandfather was sitting quietly beside the fire, with his hat pulled down over his eyes. He had his thumbs hooked into his waistcoat pockets and his legs stretched out in front of him. He had been listening to everything that was said, but at these last words, he sat up straight in his chair, pushed his hat to the back of his head and shouted out, 'Give up my pipe? Give up my pipe? I won't give up my pipe! I've been smoking that pipe since I was going to school! In fact,' he continued, warming to the subject, 'if I remember myself right, when I was a little baby in the cradle I used to take a puff out of that pipe after my morning bottle!'

I might have mentioned to you before about my grandfather. He didn't tell lies, but sometimes he was a bit careless with the truth. This might have been one of those times.

Anyway, as if to prove his point beyond any doubt, he pulled out his big, old, curved Captain Peterson pipe, filled it up with tobacco, tamped it down carefully and put a match to it. With the blue smoke billowing about him, he stared defiantly around the kitchen, daring anyone to object. 'Now, Doctor O'Halloran!' he said in a triumphant voice. 'Will I give up my pipe?'

Of course the doctor couldn't answer, because he was gone, but my mother held up two floury hands and appealed to my father, who had been sitting at the other side of the fire all this time, reading a newspaper. 'D'you see that?' she cried. 'He's trying to do away with himself!'

'Do away with myself?' repeated Grandfather, biting the end of his pipe stem. 'I'll do away with Doctor O'Halloran! That's what I'll do, if he doesn't keep his nose out of my business!'

Very slowly, my father folded up his newspaper and placed it on the floor beside him. He looked at my mother, and from her to Grandfather, and he gave a little sigh. 'I'm of a mind,' he said at last, 'that there's too much in this world of people telling other people what they should and shouldn't do. If he wants to smoke his pipe, let him!' That put an end to that.

'Any news of Katie?' I asked after a bit, by way of changing the subject.

'The poor girl is much the same,' answered my mother. 'I've made up a little package for you to take over there after supper. Mr McCafferty is working away down near the river for John Sullivan, so he won't be there. But don't delay too long, just in case he comes home early.'

As soon as I had finished my supper, I tucked the little parcel under my arm and struck off across our lower meadow, which was the short cut if you were heading for the McCaffertys' house. There was a hedge at the far side of the meadow, and I knew a place where I could get through it without too much trouble. As I did so, two magpies hopped out of a bush and flew away, chattering angrily to each other. That made me feel good because, as everyone knows, two magpies together is a good sign. Maybe my wish for Katie was going to come true after all, I thought.

But it's surprising how quickly things can change. By the time I had crossed the next field, I was pretty well convinced that any luck travelling with me was going to be bad. The first thing that made me think so was a raven, which flew over my head and croaked. That was a bad enough sign, but there was worse to come. As I stepped over the stone ditch which bordered the field, I came across the worst bad-luck sign you can get: a devil's coach-horse.

I don't know if you've ever seen a devil's coach-horse, but if you keep your eyes open in the countryside during the summer, you're pretty sure to come across one sooner or later. He's a long, black beetle, with two long, curved jaws. If he sees you, he spreads those jaws wide and curls his tail up over his back. When he does that, he's putting the evil eye on you. The only way to fend off the curse is to get the heel of your shoe down on him as fast as you can, and then spit three times on what's left of him.

I knew that, and I tried to do it, but just as I did, a stone slipped under my shoe and I missed my mark. The coach-horse had done what he wanted to do, and he decided there wouldn't be much profit in standing around any longer. As quick as lightning, he slipped down between the stones and out of sight. I put my package on the ground and pulled the stones apart, hoping to come at him, but it was no good. He was gone.

I sat down on the edge of the ditch and scratched my head. What would happen next, I wondered.

'Well,' I said aloud at last, getting up, 'things can't get much worse!' And, tucking the parcel back under my arm, I trotted off across the third and last field which would bring me out into the McCaffertys' farmyard.

(3)

KATIE McCAFFERTY

The McCaffertys' farmyard was small and cluttered. The outhouses leaning up against the house looked ready to tumble down at any moment, and all the roofs sagged in the middle. That was because the timbers holding them up were rotten, and the McCaffertys were too poor to replace them.

There was a big pile of junk in one corner of the yard: old rusty ploughs, pieces of broken mowing-machines, old buckets without handles and empty bottles by the score. In another corner was an old ramshackle pigsty, and when the pig inside heard me walking in the yard, he put his snout to the bottom of the door and started grunting. I was tempted to open the door to see if he had a knot in his tail, but I didn't. Beside the pigsty was a big clump of stinging nettles, and a few scrawny old hens were wandering in and out around there, scratching for worms. By the look of them, they didn't get much else to eat.

The door of the house was open, so I stuck my head in and said, 'Hello!'

'Hello, yourself!' a voice came back. 'Is that you, Jimmy?'

Mrs McCafferty came out of a side room, pulling the door closed behind her. She was a tall, thin woman, with a pair of spectacles perched on the end of her nose. She never looked through them, but always peered at you over the rims.

'Good day, Mrs McCafferty,' I said. 'I've come to see Katie.'

She gave a little sigh and passed her hand across her forehead. 'You're right welcome, Jimmy. And she'll be glad to see you. But don't stay too long; the doctor said she's to get as much rest as possible.' While she was talking, she glanced once or twice at the parcel under my arm. I stepped forward and set it gingerly on the table. When I looked up, she was staring at me, and her eyes were all shiny. It made me feel sort of embarrassed and uncomfortable.

'My mother sent this,' I murmured.

Mrs McCafferty picked it up from the table and, without a word, slipped it into a little cupboard and closed the door. 'God will reward her for her kindness,' she said quietly, more to herself than to me. 'Go along, now,' she went on, 'go in and see Katie. I'll make you a cup of tea.'

'Don't worry about the tea, Mrs McCafferty,' I said. 'I won't be staying that long. I don't want to tire Katie out.' That was true, but the main reason why I didn't intend to stay was that I knew I was carrying bad luck with me. It was enough for poor Katie to be sick without me bringing bad luck to her.

I opened the door of the room Mrs McCafferty had come out of, and went in quietly. Katie was sitting up in the bed, propped up by a couple of pillows behind her back. She looked pale and tired, and she was staring fixedly at the window when I went in. When she heard the door open, she looked across at me and smiled, but I thought the smile looked a bit forced – at least, the part you could see did. It's sort of hard to explain, but I've always thought that there are two sides to a smile: there's the outside, which is the part you see, and there's the inside, which you don't see. The outside of Katie's smile was forced, as though it took a great effort, but the inside was real enough – you could

tell by the way her eyes lit up that she was glad to see me.

I sat down beside her bed. 'Hello, Katie. How are you feeling?'

'Oh, I'm pretty good, Jimmy,' she answered, 'except that my chest hurts a bit. The doctor says I can get up next week, if the weather stays fine.'

We chatted on for about ten minutes or so. I told her all about how I got into trouble with Mr O'Shea at school, and what Mikey McGrory said should be done to him. That made her laugh, but in the middle of the laugh she got a terrible fit of coughing and couldn't get her breath. I was going to call her mother, but Katie put out her hand and stopped me. After a minute she was all right again, but she looked very shaken.

'Myself and Mikey went down to Hegarty's old wishing-well,' I said, after a bit.

'Did you?' she said. 'I wish I could go. I love that old place. Did you make a wish?'

I nodded.

'What was it?' she asked.

I very nearly told her, but at the last second I bit my tongue. 'You know I can't tell you that, Katie.

It wouldn't come true if I did.'

'I know,' she said, her eyes twinkling. 'I'm only teasing.'

After a bit longer, I got up to go. 'Well, Katie,' I said, 'I'll be getting along. I'll come to see you again tomorrow, or the day after.'

'Do that, Jimmy. It's nice to have someone to talk to.'

I said goodbye and went out to the kitchen. As I closed the door of Katie's room, I heard her start another fit of coughing.

Mrs McCafferty was sitting with her elbows on the table, her chin cupped in her hands. She looked at me and raised her eyebrows.

'She looks a bit better, I think, Mrs McCafferty,' I said, as cheerfully as I could.

Mrs McCafferty made no answer to that. She just shook her head slowly. 'Run along now, Jimmy,' she said. 'Thank your mother for the parcel.'

There was a strange sort of feeling in that house that evening, and I was glad to be out of it – though I was sorry, too, to see Katie looking so poorly. Despite what I'd said to Mrs McCafferty, she hadn't looked at all well.

I hopped over the ditch into the field and headed for the spot where I had seen the devil's coach-horse. The bad luck hadn't appeared yet, but I knew it was only a matter of time. The question was: what form would it take?

WISHES DON'T COME TRUE

The next afternoon, my mother paid a visit to the McCafferty house, and the news she brought back wasn't too encouraging. Katie had taken a turn for the worse during the night and was sicker than ever.

I wanted to go and see her, but my mother stopped me. 'You can't go, Jimmy, she's not allowed visitors, and besides, she's asleep most of the time now.'

That didn't sound good, and, no matter how hard I tried, I couldn't shake off the feeling that it was all my fault. I should never have called to see her with the bad luck from the devil's coach-horse on me. It was all preying heavily on my mind, and the first chance I got to talk to Grandfather alone, I told him my story.

We were standing outside together, leaning on the gate of the lower meadow, and he listened silently to every word I said. When I'd finished, he stood there for a while, staring out over the gate, saying nothing.

After a while, he spat into the field and turned towards me. 'Now listen, Jimmy, and listen carefully. No matter what you did, or what you saw, Katie McCafferty being sick has nothing in the world to do with you. Katie's illness has been with her since the day she was born. Her father and mother both know it and, what's more, they know she's not going to recover. And all that nonsense about the devil's coach-horse is just that: nonsense. The devil's coach-horse is just a beetle, plain and simple. There's no more evil in him than there is in a honeybee.'

'What about the wish I made at Hegarty's well?' I asked. 'Won't that work for Katie?'

Grandfather shrugged. 'All the wishes under the sun won't help poor Katie McCafferty now, Jimmy. I'm afraid she hasn't long to live.'

Well, that was small comfort to me. But in a way I felt a little better knowing that I wasn't the cause of Katie's being worse.

On Monday morning I met Mikey McGrory outside the school gates. The first thing I said was, 'What about your wish?'

'Don't talk about it!' he said with a snort. 'That old well of Hegarty's should be filled in. Its wishes are worse when they come true than when they don't! I wished for a catapult. And guess what? I was fooling around in our hayshed and I found one stuck behind a rafter. A beauty, too – made from an ash branch, and the straps cut from the tube of a motorbike tyre. "My wish come true!" I said. I went out into the yard to try it, and the first stone I fired broke the kitchen window and knocked the fork out of my father's hand just as he was putting a spud in his mouth! I had to run for my life! The catapult was thrown in the fire, and I have to pay for the broken window. But I'll tell you something,' he added with a wink, 'I'm going down to Hegarty's tonight to get my penny back. When I throw a penny in a well, I expect value for money.'

Well, it was hard to blame him for being sour, and I didn't think much of the well myself, come to that. It hadn't done anything for me either. So I made my mind up that I would go along with Mikey that evening and get my threepenny bit back.

The bell rang just then and we had to go in to lessons, and it certainly wasn't wells or wishes that were bothering me for the rest of the day. Mr O'Shea had decided that we should all learn the capital cities of Europe. I could remember Dublin all right, and London, and even Paris, but that was it. The rest of them just wouldn't stay put for me. After a lot of effort I got Warsaw settled in Poland, Helsinki in Finland, and Vienna in Austria. But when Mr O'Shea asked me to stand up and say them out, somehow or other I had moved Warsaw to Austria, and Helsinki to Poland, and for the life of me I couldn't remember where I had left Vienna.

'Sit down,' he said to me at last, 'and give up any hopes you might have had of becoming an airline pilot – you'd never find your way.' I didn't know what he meant by that, but some of the girls started giggling, so I supposed it was his idea of a joke.

When school was over, Mikey and myself set off once again for Hegarty's place. The weekend had been dry, which was ideal for haymaking, so now the crop was secured and the roadside meadows were empty of men. Rows of haycocks stood in the fields, like great golden thimbles, each topped off with a square of white cloth to help throw off any rain that might fall.

But we hadn't got very far when we met Mikey's mother coming along the road towards us. 'Well, boys?' she greeted us. 'And where are you off to?'

'We're just going down to Hegarty's old well, Mrs McGrory,' I answered.

She stood in the middle of the road and put her hands on her hips. 'Well now, Jimmy McElhatton,' she said, '*you* might be going down to Hegarty's well, but Mikey McGrory isn't going any such place! He's going home this minute to help his father clean out the hayshed, to be ready for drawing in the hay.'

Mikey scratched his head, looked at his mother, and looked at me. 'I'll have to go,' he said quietly. 'Do me a favour, get my penny for me, will you?'

I nodded. 'I will.'

(5)

HEGARTY

Well, if it was possible for Hegarty's place to look more lonesome than it had before, it looked it that evening. I expect the fact that I was on my own had a lot to do with it, but even allowing for that, there seemed to be something *extra*-lonely about it this time. You know how I said before that it seemed like an empty church? Well, this time it seemed more like a graveyard.

The trees surrounding the place seemed to have grown closer together, and their tops were leaning against one another as though they were chatting silently. And if there was anything else around that was chatting, it was doing it silently too, because there wasn't a sound. You would have heard a pin drop. Even the water that was trickling away from the well was doing it in perfect silence.

I thought for a moment that I must have gone deaf, but I found out this wasn't the case by saying out loud, 'James McElhatton!' And for once in my life, I was glad to hear the sound of that name – except it seemed *too* loud, somehow, and I was half afraid to say it again. I had this awful feeling that someone was staring at me, and it gave me the shivers.

I looked around from side to side, over my head and behind my back, but there was no one there. I decided it was just my nerves getting the better of me.

'I've come this far,' I muttered under my breath, 'and whatever happens, I'm not going away without my threepenny bit – and Mikey's penny, for that matter!' Saying that sort of braced up my courage.

I went forward to the well and knelt down beside the black slab with the strange mark on it. I rolled up my sleeve and dipped my hand into the well. The water was as cold as ice, and it made me pause for a second. The old story came back to my mind, about the man who had tried to take his money back, and I had a vision of a hand shooting up and pulling me down into the depths of the well. But I thought of what Grandfather had told me about those old superstitions and, gritting my teeth,

I shoved my hand in deeper.

I could see my threepenny bit shining among the other coins at the bottom, but I couldn't quite reach it. So I pulled my hand out and rolled my sleeve up further. Then, lying down flat on the edge of the black stone, I reached in deeper.

My fingers were just closing around the little coin when, all of a sudden, there was a tremendous splash, and before I got a chance to do anything, another hand gripped mine, under the water! I let out a shriek of terror, and a horrible blackness came over me.

I awoke to find myself lying on my back, staring up at the sky. At first I didn't know where I was, but then it came back to me and I realised I must have fainted.

I sat up. There in front of me, squatting on her heels and staring at me, was a young woman. She was dressed in a white shirt, faded grey trousers and a pair of soft leather shoes. A thick shock of black hair hung down over one shoulder, and her eyes were the brightest, most startling blue you could imagine. She was very beautiful – kind of dazzling, in fact. I couldn't say how old she was, she was much older than me, but at the same time, she somehow seemed to be sort of young.

'That was a foolish thing you tried to do,' she said, smiling at me.

'What?' I asked with a gasp.

'You tried to take a coin out of the well. Don't you know what happened to the last person who tried that?'

'I don't believe that old rubbish!' I said stoutly, sounding a lot braver than I felt. 'And anyway, who are you?'

She plucked a blade of grass from beside the well and began to chew it. 'I'm the person who stopped you,' she said after a bit, looking at me with a sort of laugh in her eyes, if you get my meaning. 'If I hadn't grabbed your hand in time...' she went on, shaking her head. 'Very foolish thing you tried. Very.'

'What was foolish about it?' I demanded. 'Wishes don't come true from this old well.'

She interrupted me by placing a finger on her lips. 'Some do, and some don't,' she whispered.

'Well, any of the ones I know about haven't,' I said sullenly. I got to my feet and stared at her uneasily. 'Who are you?' I asked again.

She stood up. 'My name doesn't matter,' she said, holding out her hand as though she wanted me to shake it. 'But I'm pleased to meet you!'

Gingerly I stretched out my hand and shook hers lightly. 'My name is Jimmy.'

We stood there for a moment, staring at each other. She looked as though she was going to start laughing at any moment, and whatever was in it, I found myself smiling too! I just couldn't help it!

'Well,' I said at last, 'I'd better be getting home. They'll be expecting me.'

'You do that,' she said, still smiling her curious smile, 'and don't worry any more about your wish. If it's meant to come true, never fear, it will.'

There was something strange about her that I couldn't put my finger on. But the longer I stayed near her, the more I felt as though I wanted to be somewhere else. So I didn't waste any time putting some distance between us.

Just as I turned the bend of the laneway that would hide me from her view, I glanced back. I felt sure that she would be watching me, but I was wrong. She was stooping down in front of the well, and she was tracing the strange mark on the stone with her finger. It made a picture that gave me that funny, prickly feeling at the back of my neck again, and I got out of there as quick as I could.

(6)

JULIA

I was intending to tell everyone about the strange woman I'd met as soon as I got home, but when I marched into the house with my story on my lips, I got a surprise that shut me up before I even got started: Julia McGrory.

Julia was Mikey's sister. She had red hair like her brother's, only instead of being spiky like Mikey's, it was long and twisted into plaits. She was a year younger than me, and she was a pain in the neck. She was always hanging around our house, and she used to make a habit of following me around the school yard – so much so that people were beginning to say she was my *girlfriend*, which she wasn't! And she was always asking me to tell her stories and...well, and a hundred other annoying things. Everyone said she was pretty and clever, and I suppose she was, but I just wished she'd leave me alone.

'Look who's here!' said my mother. 'It's Julia!'

Well, I could see that. It wasn't as if she was hiding under the table. She was sitting next to the fireplace, drinking a glass of lemonade and grinning at me. 'Hello, Jimmy!' she said.

I didn't say anything. I just clumped up to the table and sat down.

Grandfather was sitting by the fire, opposite Julia, and he wasn't taking Dr O'Halloran's advice – he was driving smoke up out of his pipe like a steam engine.

'Julia was just telling us,' he said, between puffs, 'about how you were kept back after school on Friday for disrupting the lesson.'

Well! Wasn't that just like Julia? What a blabbermouth! I glared at her, but she just smiled back and took another sip of her lemonade.

Just then, my father came in. He hung his cap on a nail on the back of the door and said 'Hello!' to Julia.

'Here, now!' said my mother, coming over to the table with a big plate of boiled potatoes. 'Supper's ready. You might as well stay and have a bite, Julia, since you're here.'

'Thank you, Mrs McElhatton,' said Julia. 'I'm not very hungry, but I won't refuse.'

And with that, she got up and plonked herself down at the table, right next to me. And even though she'd said she wasn't hungry, she still managed to pack away a plate of salt pork and cabbage, and three or four floury spuds.

When supper was finished, my father told me to go out and weed the cabbage garden. Even though I wasn't too fond of weeding, I was glad of the excuse to get away. But it was no use – Julia got up and said she'd go with me. She'd help, she said.

And off we went, the two of us, to weed the cabbage. And Julia did help, that is, if standing around watching someone weed cabbage counts as helping. It wouldn't have been so bad if she'd kept quiet, but she kept on and on with, 'What's the name of that weed?' and 'What's the name of that one?'

After a bit, I said, 'Don't you have to be getting home, Julia? Won't your mother be worried about you?'

'Oh, no,' she answered, 'she knows where I am.' Then she said, 'Tell me a story.'

'I don't know any,' I said, pulling up a fistful of weeds.

'Yes, you do. Tell me the one about the Leprechaun.'

I straightened myself up and put my hands on my hips. 'You already heard that one, Julia. I told it to you before – and you didn't believe it!'

'Well, tell me again,' she insisted. 'Maybe I will this time!'

And she kept on and on until, in the end, for the sake of peace, I had to tell her the whole rigmarole over again about an adventure I had had with a Leprechaun.

By the time I'd got to the end of the story, the evening was nearly gone. The sky had turned a dark blue-grey and you could see an odd early star appearing here and there. Away in the west, the sun was sinking into a sea of red, and a blackbird was calling 'Dig!dig!dig!' as he headed for his bed. The ghostly shape of a woodcock flew past, setting out on his nightly wanderings, and I looked at the cabbage with a frown. What with explaining things to Julia and telling her the story, I hadn't got even half of it weeded, but it was too late to do any more.

'We'd better be getting back,' I said, and we set off homeward. When we arrived, I got a jarring from my mother for keeping Julia out so late. Keeping Julia out! Wasn't that a good one? After me telling her to go home hours before!

We each got a cup of milk and a slice of bread and butter, and then my father said, 'It's too late for Julia to be out on her own; you'd better walk home with her. And mind you come straight back.'

'Thank you, Mr McElhatton,' said Julia, smiling her silly smile. 'And don't worry, I'll send him straight home.'

When she said that, they all looked at me and started laughing. And wasn't I mad! If Julia hadn't been a girl, and a year younger than me, I would have kicked her! Telling them *she'd* send *me* home!

7

A WOMAN IN THE DARK

The road we had to walk down to get to Julia's house was very narrow. Tall ash trees grew along either side, and where the sky showed between them, you could see bats fluttering over our heads. Julia was saying nothing, for a change. I think she was frightened of the bats. I was tempted to tell her about the woman I'd met down at Hegarty's well, just for something to talk about, but I knew if I did she'd plague me with questions, so I kept my mouth shut.

Halfway along the road, we had to cross a little footbridge which spanned the river, and as we approached it, I could see in the dusk that there was someone standing on it. I thought at first that it might be Mikey, or his father, coming to meet Julia, but when we got a bit nearer I could tell it wasn't either of them. It was a woman with long hair, and she was just standing on the bridge, looking down into the water.

Julia and I said nothing as we stepped onto the bridge, but as we did, the woman turned towards us and said 'Good evening'. I got a bit of a start then, because she looked just like the woman I'd seen down at the well, except that her hair, instead of being black, was red. When she spoke, she smiled, but it wasn't a friendly smile – at least, that was how it seemed to me. It was the sort of smile that a person gets when he sees a cream cake in front of him and is thinking about eating it. It gave me the shivers!

'Good evening,' Julia and I replied together, and we walked on over the bridge. While we were crossing, Julia had taken hold of my hand, and I hadn't noticed. I did now, and I shook it loose.

'Who's she?' Julia whispered, when we were out of earshot.

'How do I know?' I answered, looking back over my shoulder. 'I expect she's a tourist.'

'A *tourist*? Standing alone on the bridge? At this hour? What's she doing there?'

'Well, *I* don't know,' I said irritably. 'Your guess is as good as mine.'

'There was something weird about her,' said Julia with a shiver. 'She gave me the creeps!'

Before long, we reached the mouth of the little boreen which led up to Julia's house. I peered along the length of it. The lights of the house were shining out through the open door and the windows.

'You'll be all right on your own from here,' I said.

'I will, of course,' said Julia. 'Thanks for seeing me home, Jimmy. I wouldn't have liked to meet *her* on my own. Will you be all right?'

Now, as it happens, I wasn't looking forward at all to passing the woman again. Like Julia had said, there was something weird about her. It crossed my mind to ask Julia to tell Mikey to come out to me, but she was so smart I knew she'd realise I was afraid, and I couldn't give her that satisfaction. So I said, 'What d'you mean? Of course I'll be all right. She's only a woman – she's not going to *eat* me!' And with that, I turned on my heel and marched off grimly.

It was dark by now, but the moon was just coming up, and you could make out the road and the dark shapes of the trees easily enough. I whistled a little tune under my breath as I walked along. By the time I got near the bridge, the moon had lifted clear of the mountaintop, and it was plenty bright enough for me to see that there was no one on the bridge. I breathed a sigh of relief. The woman was gone.

Or so I thought.

Just when I was about ten yards short of the bridge, she appeared on the other side. I stopped and watched her. She walked up onto the bridge and just stood there. Then she reached behind her and took something out of her pocket. I didn't know what it was at first, but I soon saw that it was a comb, because she began running it through her hair.

The moonlight was shining down on her, casting an eerie shadow on the ground, and as she combed her hair, she hummed a tune. The whole scene looked odd, and I felt my scalp sort of tightening, as if my hair was standing on end.

But I couldn't stand there all night, so I took a deep breath and walked boldly forward. As I came up to her, she stopped her combing and stood to one side to let me pass.

'You're out late,' she said.

'I am, I suppose,' I said, glancing at her, and as I did so, I stumbled.

'Watch out!' she said.

'I'm okay,' I gasped, gathering myself.

At that, she gave a throaty chuckle. 'That's not what I meant.'

'What, then?' I asked.

She took a step towards me and put her hand on my shoulder. When she did that, a cold shudder went through me. And then she stooped forward and put her mouth close to my ear and said in a horrible, hissing whisper, 'People who poke their noses in other people's business often find themselves in trouble!' And she smiled that awful cake-eating smile again. 'Now get along, *Mr Well-wisher*!'

You may be sure she didn't have to tell me twice! I took to my heels and never drew breath till I got to my own house and put the front door between me and the night.

When I rushed in, they all looked at me. There were teacups on the table and my mother was pouring tea into them. 'You're in a hurry,' she said, raising her eyebrows at me.

Grandfather was sitting by the fire, smoking his

pipe. 'What happened you?' he said. 'You look as though you'd seen a ghost!'

My father looked at me over the top of the paper he was reading. 'Maybe Julia tried to kiss him,' he said with a smirk, and they all started smiling.

'She did no such thing!' I protested, but they just kept on smiling away to one another.

I drank a cup of tea in silence, and soon after, I was tucked up in bed. But sleep didn't come to me for a long time after, and when it did, it was an uneasy sleep, and I thought at one stage that I heard a strange cry in the night.

8

GRANDFATHER EXPLAINS

The next day was Tuesday, but there was no school because Mr O'Shea had to go to a wedding. I heard them arguing even before I got up – my mother and Grandfather. Their words came drifting up the stairs to me, but I couldn't hear rightly what it was all about until I came down to my breakfast, and even then I couldn't seem to understand it.

'And I tell you she *was* in being,' Grandfather was saying, 'and, what's more, she still *is* in being! I *heard* her!'

My mother tossed her head as she laid a couple of rashers in the frying-pan. 'Old people used to be going on with that nonsense when I was small,' she said. 'They used to be telling us those old stories so that we were afraid to go out in the dark! There never were such things!'

'There were!' insisted Grandfather. 'And there still are! I heard her, I tell you!'

As all this was going on, my father was sitting at the table, drinking a mug of tea. While the other two argued away, I sat down beside him and whispered, 'What's this about?'

'The Banshee,' he answered quietly. 'The old man thinks he heard her last night, but your mother doesn't like to talk about that kind of thing.'

I stared around at them, from one to the other. 'What *is* the Banshee?' I whispered to my father, but he only gave a sigh and shook his head, as my mother put a plate of rashers and eggs in front of me.

'Eat your breakfast, boy, before it gets cold. There's work to be done. Half the cabbage garden still needs weeding – what were you doing out there last night?'

I could see that he was going to start pulling my leg about Julia again, so I asked no more questions, only swallowed my breakfast as fast as I could.

As soon as I'd finished, I headed off out to the cabbage garden. It was fine and quiet out there, just the sounds of the birds singing and flies droning overhead, and I worked away contentedly at the weeds. Now and then, I would come across a little cluster of yellow eggs on a cabbage leaf, and I would have to crush those with my thumb, because if they were left, they'd hatch into caterpillars – they can eat cabbage faster than people do!

It must have been around midday when I realised Grandfather was nearby. I smelled the tobacco smoke from his pipe before I saw him walking towards me. My mother had sent him to me with some bread and butter and a bottle of milk for my lunch. I sat down on the verge of the ditch and munched away while he smoked his pipe.

'Grandfather,' I said, with my mouth full of bread, 'what is the Banshee?'

'Hrrmph!' he grunted, blowing out a big cloud of smoke. 'According to your mother, it's just a superstition!'

I took a swallow of milk from the bottle. 'But what is it according to *you*?'

He took the pipe out of his mouth, closed one eye against the sun and squinted at me. 'If you're really interested, I'll tell you,' he said. 'But,' he added, pointing at me with the stem of his pipe, 'I don't expect you'll believe me either.'

I finished my milk and sat back expectantly. Grandfather sat down beside me, pushed his cap to

the back of his head, stuck his pipe between his teeth, and began to talk out of the side of his mouth.

'The word Banshee comes from the Irish *bean-sidhe*, which means fairy-woman. But what we refer to as the Banshee is a special type of fairy-woman. She comes around only when someone is about to die, and even then, only for special people – people from certain families. She is a bringer of death.'

'What is she like?' I asked, very excited.

He considered.

'People don't usually see her – they just hear her. She cries and screeches in the dead of night, and when she does, someone nearby is marked for death.'

He paused and narrowed his eyes, as if he were straining to see into the distance. 'I remember,' he went on, 'when my own grandfather died. She came then–'

'What d'you mean?' I interrupted. 'How d'you mean, she *came*? Where did she come to?'

'She just *came*,' he said with a shrug. 'We didn't see her, but we heard her right enough.'

I was going to ask what exactly he'd heard, but he'd narrowed his eyes again and I realised that the distance he was staring into was the distance of the past. So I kept quiet.

After a moment, he carried on. 'We were walking home late one night, my father and myself. We'd been visiting old Jimmy McGrory – that'd be your friend's great-great-grandfather. And when we came near the house, my father stopped and grabbed me by the arm. He asked me if I could hear something. I said I couldn't, and he told me to listen more carefully. And then I did hear it. It was like a child crying in the distance, very faint at first, but soon it got louder, and louder, till it was like a terrible scream. And then it gradually faded away again into the distance. I didn't know what it was, but it frightened the life out of me. I asked my father what it was, but he just told me to pay no attention – that it was nothing for me to worry about.'

With that, Grandfather shook his head, spat on the ground, stuck his pipe back in his mouth and began puffing away again.

'But what happened *then*?' I demanded.

'What happened?' he repeated. 'Nothing happened. We went home and my grandfather died the very next day. And it wasn't too many months after,' he added, in a quiet, grim voice, 'that I heard that cry again, only this time it was for my father.'

He stood up and picked up the empty milk-bottle. I begged him to tell me more, but he only said, 'You'd better finish your weeding. We can talk later. I have other things to do now.'

And he stomped off across the garden, puffing smoke as he went.

After he'd gone, I went back to my weeding, but my mind wasn't really on the job. I was thinking about what he'd told me, and all kinds of awful thoughts were going through my mind. What a terrible thing it would be, I thought, to hear that awful cry, and to know that someone was going to die.

And then another thought crossed my mind: what if you knew someone who was sick, and then you heard the Banshee? You would know almost for sure that that person was marked for death, and then what would you do?

When I thought of that, I pulled a young cabbage plant out of the ground by mistake, instead of a weed, because it had just struck me: Katie McCafferty was *very* sick, and Grandfather had heard the Banshee last night!

9

MONEY BACK

By the time I'd finished weeding, it was suppertime, and I wasn't sorry. I had a pain in my back from stooping, and my hands were sore where I had grabbed a stinging nettle without realising it.

For supper we had mutton stew, which was a favourite of mine, and I was so busy packing it into myself that for a moment I didn't realise that Grandfather wasn't sitting at the table. I glanced around the kitchen, but he was nowhere to be seen.

'He's gone upstairs for a rest,' my father explained. 'He has a touch of a sore chest.'

'If he doesn't give up that pipe, it'll be the death of him,' said my mother.

'Don't start that again,' said my father with a sigh. 'He's old enough to know himself.'

We ate away in silence for a bit, and then my mother said, 'Poor Katie McCafferty is very low. They don't think there's much hope.'

That made me feel bad. Together with Grand-father not feeling well, it seemed like there was a cloud over everything. I was glad when there was the sound of a footstep outside the door and Mikey McGrory walked in. I finished up my supper and strolled outside with him.

I had been meaning to go up and talk to Grand-father, but Mikey had other ideas.

'Did you get it?' he asked.

'Get what?'

'My money! What else?'

I'd forgotten all about that. 'I didn't,' I said, 'nor my threepence either.' And I went on to tell him all about what had happened down at the well.

As I was talking, I could see a sort of scornful look come into his eyes.

'And d'you mean to tell me,' he said when I'd finished, 'that you let some *girl* stop you from getting our money back?'

'She wasn't a girl,' I objected, 'she was a woman. And it wasn't that she actually *stopped* me – although I suppose she did – but she just made me feel that it was the wrong thing to do.'

'Huh! It might be the wrong thing for you, but

I'm going down there right now for my penny. Are you coming?'

I shook my head. 'I don't think we should.'

'Fair enough,' he said, walking away, 'if you're that scared.'

I stood thinking for a moment. 'Hold on!' I called after him. 'I'll come.' What else could I do?

I didn't feel much like talking as we walked along towards Hegarty's place, but Mikey couldn't be stopped. It occurred to me that that was something he had in common with his sister.

'Did you hear about Katie McCafferty?' he asked.

'Yes,' I said, 'I heard she's pretty sick.'

I was going to say more, but just at that moment Mikey saw a mouse at the side of the road and ran off trying to catch it. That's the kind of thing he was always doing. Anyway, the mouse was too good for him, and when he came back – before I could say anything – he said, 'I hear you walked Julia home last night.' And he plastered a silly grin across his face.

'If that's all you have to talk about,' I said, 'you'd do better to keep quiet.'

'Don't get ratty!' he said, laughing. 'I didn't mean anything! It's just that she told me there was a woman standing on the bridge. Who was she, I wonder?'

'I don't know,' I replied, glad to get the conversation away from Julia. 'She was weird. She was just standing there, combing her hair, of all things!'

Mikey gave a long, low whistle, and his next words stopped me dead in my tracks, 'Maybe she was the Banshee!'

I stared at him. 'What?' I whispered.

He stared back at me. 'What's the matter? Are you all right? You've turned white!'

'What did you say?' I croaked. 'About the B-Banshee?'

Mikey burst out laughing. 'Didn't you ever hear that the Banshee is supposed to sit by a bridge, combing her hair? Your woman fits the bill pretty well, don't you think? Ho, ho! Don't worry! I won't let her get you!' And between laughs, he gave out a long, wailing cry, 'WOOOOOOOOOOOAAAAAAA!'

But it wasn't funny to me. '*Stop it*!' I shouted.

He stopped and looked at me. 'It's only a joke, Jimmy,' he said. 'There's not really any such thing!'

'You don't know whether there is or not!' I snapped. 'Don't talk about it any more!'

'All right,' said Mikey, raising his eyebrows and opening his eyes wide. 'Keep your hair on!'

My mind was in a whirl as we passed down Hegarty's boreen. Was that woman the Banshee? If she was, what was she doing there? And if she wasn't, who was she? I couldn't think straight, and to make matters worse, Mikey kept chattering away as usual. I wasn't taking notice of anything he was saying, and there was no one else around to listen to him, but that didn't stop him. He just loved the sound of his own voice.

Before I knew it, we had arrived in Hegarty's yard and were standing in front of the well.

'D'you want to do the honours?' Mikey asked.

I shook my head. 'No. And I want you to leave my coin in there. Take out your own if you want, but leave mine.'

Mikey shrugged. 'Suit yourself!'

He rolled up his sleeve, and I stepped back to give him some room as he lay down on his stomach. Gingerly, he slipped his arm down into the water, staring down into the depths, with his tongue sticking out on one side of his mouth. Then, suddenly, he started kicking his legs up and down and screamed out, 'AAAH! *Let go! Let go!*'

I ran forward and grabbed his feet and started to pull him away from the well. But as I did so, I heard him giggling. I let go of him, and he rolled over onto his back. He was holding a shiny penny in his hand and killing himself laughing.

10

SURPRISE AT McCAFFERTYS'

Needless to say, I wasn't too impressed with Mikey McGrory's idea of a joke, and I left him in no doubt as to what I thought of him. Normally, I would have seen the funny side of it, I suppose, but just then I wasn't in the mood. I was feeling bad about Katie, and seeing as the evening was still young, I decided to stroll over that way and see if there was any news. I didn't expect to get to see her, but I thought I might find out how she was.

As I was walking along the road, a car pulled up alongside me, and who should it be but Dr O'Halloran. He asked me where I was headed, and when I told him, he said, 'I'm going there myself. Hop in and I'll give you a lift.' In I sat.

'I just called to see your grandfather, Jimmy,' he said, as he steered slowly along the road, trying to avoid the potholes.

'How is he?' I asked.

'Well, he's not too bad, I suppose, considering his age, but he'd be a lot better if he'd stop smoking that pipe.'

I nodded. 'I expect you're right, Doctor, but I don't think that's a thing he's going to do.'

The doctor pursed his lips and frowned, and we drove the rest of the way in silence. Before long, we rattled into the McCaffertys' yard, and Dr O'Halloran switched off the engine.

'You'd better stay here, young fellow,' he said, reaching behind and lifting a bag from the back seat, 'while I go in and see how she is.'

With that, he got out of the car and marched into the house, tapping on the open door with his knuckles as he went in. I did as he'd told me and stayed sitting in the car. Swallows were hawking up and down the yard for flies, and a dozen or so of them were sitting on the ridge of the house, twittering away noisily to one another. A big red and black butterfly was fluttering back and forth over the stinging nettles, and the scrawny old hens were still scratching around amongst the junk.

Normally, I would have found all those things

interesting enough to watch, but now I barely noticed them. All I could think about was Katie and the woman on the bridge. Who was she? And what had she meant by what she'd said to me? My brain was addled – it was like it was going around in circles.

Just as I was thinking all this, I heard a voice say, 'Hello, Jimmy!'

I glanced up and there was Mr McCafferty, leaning on the edge of the car window, smiling at me. He had walked up to the car without me seeing him. I couldn't believe my eyes. In all the years I'd known him, I'd never seen him smile before. One of his front teeth was missing. I'd never known that till then.

'Hello, Mr McCafferty,' I said.

'Aren't you coming in?' he asked.

'The doctor asked me to wait here until he's finished looking at Katie,' I explained.

Mr McCafferty looked towards the house. 'Well,' he said with a grin, 'that shouldn't take long.' And he walked towards the house, whistling softly to himself.

I stared after him. He was acting very strangely,

I thought. The Mr McCafferty I knew was a sad, silent man. This one looked as though he was going to start singing and dancing a jig any minute. It was as if something had affected his mind – something like...

Suddenly I felt cold. I leaned out the window and called after him, 'Mr McCafferty, how's...how's Katie?'

He stopped and looked back at me. 'Katie? Katie is – you'll see for yourself!' And he walked in the door of the house. Just at that second, Dr O'Halloran was coming out, they collided, and Mr McCafferty came staggering back.

'Ho, Doctor!' he said with a chuckle. 'You nearly did me an injury! Still, I daresay it wouldn't take you long to put me right again, eh? Ho, ho! Well, now, what do you think of our little patient today?'

Dr O'Halloran pulled out his handkerchief and mopped his forehead. 'I don't know what to say, John,' he said faintly. 'Naturally I'm delighted!' He stuffed his handkerchief back into his pocket and shook Mr McCafferty's hand. 'Delighted!' he repeated. 'It's amazing! Absolutely amazing!'

'Isn't it?' laughed Mr McCafferty, carrying on into the house.

Dr O'Halloran walked slowly up to the car, opened the rear door and put his bag carefully on the seat. Then he opened the driver's door and got in. For a long minute he just sat there, staring out through the windscreen. He seemed to be in a daze.

'Are you all right, Doctor?' I ventured at last.

He gave a little start at that, and looked at me. 'Yes, Jimmy, I'm fine. Fine.' He shook his head slowly. 'I would never have believed it possible.'

'How is Katie?'

'Katie?' he repeated. 'Katie is,' he paused, and then said, 'go and see.'

I got out of the car and, as the doctor drove away, I walked into the house. And there at the table, with her father on one side and her mother on the other, was Katie, sitting up straight and smiling the brightest smile I ever saw in my life!

I stood there, just looking at her, until she started laughing and said, 'Well, Jimmy, aren't you going to sit down?'

11

THE CURE

Mrs McCafferty's eyes were shining as she told the story. Every now and then, she looked at me or at her husband, but for the most part she couldn't take her eyes off Katie.

'It was just around midday,' she began. 'I'd made some soup, and I brought a bowl of it up to Katie, but the child was too weak to eat it. All she wanted was to sleep. I plumped up her pillows and came away. I was baking a cake – more to keep my mind occupied than anything else – when this woman came to the door. She asked for a drink of water, and of course I didn't refuse her. I told her to come in and sit down for a while. I offered her tea, but she would take nothing except plain water. We chatted away for a bit and, naturally enough, I started telling her about Katie and she asked if she could go in to see her. Well, she seemed so sympathetic and so understanding, that I didn't see any harm in it, so I agreed. Katie was asleep, and the woman went over and looked down at her. Then, before I knew what she was doing, she dipped her finger into the glass of water that she still had in her hand, and made a sign on the child's forehead.

'Well, I was that surprised! But before I could say anything to her, she said, "When she wakes, she'll be hungry." They're the very words! And that was that! She walked out of the room and left me there, looking after her with my mouth open!

By the time I'd gathered my wits enough to follow her out, there was no trace of her. I looked around the yard, and I even went out onto the road and looked up and down, but she'd vanished! And when I came back inside, Katie was sitting up in bed, asking for something to eat! And look at her now!' And with that, Mrs McCafferty gathered Katie into her arms and kissed her.

'I don't remember any of it!' Katie said with a laugh. 'I don't remember much at all about the last couple of days, to be honest. It seems more like a hazy dream than anything else. But when I woke up this afternoon, it was just as if I'd never been sick at all!'

'But who was the woman?' I asked.

'That's just it!' they answered in chorus, spreading their hands wide. 'We don't know!'

It was getting late then, so I said I should be getting home. I promised to come back the next day to see Katie, and got up to go.

As I went out, something occurred to me. 'Mrs McCafferty,' I said, turning back, 'what was the sign the woman made on Katie's forehead?'

'I don't know what it was, Jimmy,' she answered, looking at me over the top of her spectacles, 'but it was like this.' And she drew out a sign on the table with her finger. As she did, I felt a little thrill go through me. This is what she drew:

$$\delta$$

The sign of Hegarty's well!

12

HEGARTY AGAIN

The only word I know to describe the way I felt after leaving Katie's house is 'confused'. But that word doesn't really do justice to the way I was feeling. It was like someone had hit me on the head with a hammer and then turned me loose. There should be a big, long word with lots of corners on it to describe the state I was in, and there probably is, only I don't know it.

The more I tried to figure things out, the more mixed up it all seemed to get. I walked along with my head in a kind of spin. It was nearly dark when I reached the turnoff for my own house, and it was then that I said to myself, 'What brought me this way? I'd have been home long ago if I'd taken the short cut through the fields.'

But I knew why. The route I'd taken wasn't the quickest way home, but it was the way to Hegarty's place, and that's where I was going. In the back of my mind I knew that if I was ever going to sort things out, that was where I had to go. I wasn't sure what I expected to find there, but I just felt sort of *drawn* there – it's hard to explain.

The moon was sailing high by the time I reached the little laneway which led down to the well, and it cast funny shadows through the whitethorn trees on either side of the path. A little bird, snugly settled down for the night, said 'Cheep!' at me as I walked past, but that was the only sound I heard, except for the scrunching of the gravel under my feet. That sounded so loud and out of place that I actually started walking on tiptoe.

When I got to the yard, I stopped. The scene in front of me was sort of unearthly. The old broken-down house stood there, solid and menacing in the moonlight. It seemed almost like something alive – just lying there, waiting, looking at me. The trees all around seemed to lean in towards it, as if they were whispering to it. I could almost hear them: 'What does he want here, at this hour?'

Bats flitted across the clearing, and a little breeze sprang up and moaned through the trees. That seemed to have a voice too: 'Whooo's heeee?

Whyyyy's heee heeeeere?'

I shivered, and for a moment my courage failed me. I decided to go home to my nice, warm house, where the fire would be burning bright in the grate, and there would be cups on the table. I turned to go, but, as I did, the breeze died down. In the dead silence that followed, I gritted my teeth and said out loud, 'I'll take one look at the well, anyhow.'

I walked slowly around to the back of the old house, all the time glancing fearfully over my shoulder, until I stood in front of the well. The rays of the moon were falling full upon the surface of the little pool, so that it looked more like a sheet of polished silver than water. Even the black stone with the strange sign shone brightly in the white light. I sat down beside the stone and traced the outline of the sign with my finger.

'I thought you'd come,' said a voice, and my heart nearly stopped. In fact, it did stop, I think, but it started again just in time to stop me from falling down dead.

I jerked my head up, and there she was, looking down at me: the woman with the black hair who'd grabbed my hand the time before.

I couldn't say anything for a bit, because my tongue wouldn't work after the fright she'd given me, but after a minute I managed to say, 'It was you, wasn't it?'

She sat down on the ground beside me. 'What was me?' she asked.

'It was you who made Katie better.'

She shook her head at that. 'No, Jimmy, it was not me. It was you. It's not the hammer that drives the nail, it's the hand that holds the hammer. I was just the hammer, yours was the hand that held it.'

'Me?' I cried. 'How could it have been me? I wasn't even there!'

'Ah, but you were there! At least, a part of you was – a very important part – your wish.'

'I don't understand–' I began, but she cut me short.

'Listen,' she said, 'everybody gets a wish, Jimmy. You're born with it. It's just as much a part of you as your nose, or your ear, or your big toe. Of course, you can't see it, but it's there just the same. And after all, there are many other bits of you that you can't see either – like your heart, and your spleen, and your imagination – but you know they're there, don't you? But the only thing about the wish is that you only get to use it once. And to get it to work, you have to use it at the right time, and in the right place. You can make a hundred different wishes in a hundred different places, but they'll never come true if it's the wrong time or the wrong place.

'Your wish was a good one – for Katie McCafferty to get better – and it so happened that you wished it at the right time and in the right place: here.'

I got up onto my knees and stared at her. 'But who *are* you?' I asked.

She smiled a strange, lovely smile at that, and said, 'I'm your wish come true – that's all you need to know. And now it's time you were going, I'm expecting another visitor tonight.' And with that, she stood up and began walking slowly towards the old house.

'One thing!' I said, getting to my feet. 'Who is the other woman – the one with the red hair?'

At that she stopped. After a second, she turned and stared into my eyes. It was as if she was looking right through them, into my mind. And at that moment an expression of sadness came over her face, and for some reason I felt a lump coming in to my throat, like when you're saying goodbye to someone.

'She's who you think she is, Jimmy,' she said quietly.

'But – but,' I said, feeling cold, 'I think she's...I think she's the *Banshee*!'

She made no answer to that, just turned and walked away into the old broken-down ruin.

'Wait!' I shouted, going after her. 'Come back!'

I ran to the door of the old house, but there was no one there.

'Don't you even have a name?' I cried into the darkness.

The little breeze blew up again, and as it sighed in the trees, I heard her voice, 'I thought you'd have guessed.'

'What?' I cried. 'What is it?'

I had to strain my ears to catch the reply that came back to me on a laughing breath of wind, 'He-e-e-e-garty-y-y-y-y.'

13

BANSHEE!

I stood there, looking around me in the moonlight. 'Wake up, James McElhatton!' I said to myself. 'All this is just a dream! You're really at home, tucked up in your bed, fast asleep.' I tried pinching myself, and even slapping myself in the face, but it was all useless. I couldn't get out of it – I was still there in Hegarty's yard.

Slowly, with my hands in my pockets, I picked my way around to the front of the old ruin and began walking up the narrow little laneway which led to the road. I was thinking it all over, but it was just too much for me to understand. I decided to go home and tell it all to Grandfather, in the hope that he'd be able to explain it.

Just as I reached the end of the little laneway, a cloud drifted in front of the moon and it turned very dark for a few moments. And when it cleared, I nearly jumped out of my skin! There had been nothing in front of me a second ago, but there was someone there now, and my blood ran cold when I saw who it was: the red-haired woman!

There she stood, right in my path, grinning a horrible, triumphant grin. The breeze that had moaned in the trees a while ago returned, only stronger, and blew around her head, tangling and twisting her wild red hair. Her eyes were blazing and there were dark shadows under them, like someone who hasn't slept, and red rims around them, like someone who's been crying.

I tried to cry out, but it felt like my mouth was full of sand and my throat was closed up with fear. I wanted to run – it didn't matter where, just to get away from her – but I couldn't. My feet were rooted to the ground. So we stood there, staring at each other.

And then she said, or rather hissed, 'Hello, Mr Well-wisher!' And she reached out, grabbed me by the shirt-collar and pulled me towards her. I was so frightened I wanted to cry, but I couldn't. I couldn't do anything. I was like a big, quivering lump of jelly!

Her face was so close to me now that our noses were almost touching, and she said in a horrible, sneering voice, 'I came for Katie McCafferty, but *you* had to stick your nose in with your infernal, interfering *wish*. But I haven't given up on her yet, and maybe I'll even get a bonus! This one is special! I've waited a long time for this!'

She started laughing then – a mad laugh, terrifying to hear. And then, suddenly, she flung me away from her, and I fell in a heap against the hedge. And as I watched her, her mouth opened wider, and *wider*, and **WIDER**!

Then she turned her face towards the sky and let out the most terrible, bloodcurdling, ear-splitting, stomach-turning, mind-boggling cry that you, or I, or anybody else ever heard. It was as if all the pain and torment and anguish of a thousand years, all the lost hopes and broken dreams of a hundred ages, had all been put together in that scream.

I clapped my hands to my ears, and screwed my eyes up tight, and gritted my teeth, and rolled myself up in a ball. But it was no use, I could still hear it – piercing into my brain, roaring and throbbing in

my ears. It went on and on and on and on! It seemed as if there was no end to it.

But just when I was sure that I couldn't bear it another second, it began to get a little less loud, a little less piercing, and then it seemed to be going farther away, fainter and fainter, and ever fainter, until it was gone. I opened my eyes, and through the tears that were running out of them, I saw that she was gone too.

I scrambled to my feet. I was drenched in sweat and trembling all over. My heart was hammering under my ribs, and I had to lean against the hedge for a few minutes before I was able to start walking again. But eventually I got moving. And when I did, I didn't spare the horses, as they say. I lifted my feet and fairly flew along the road towards home.

The memory of that fearful yell was still ringing in my ears and, worse than that, a dreadful, sickening fear was gradually growing inside me. Maybe Katie McCafferty wasn't out of danger after all! And now it looked as though the Banshee was going to try for someone else as well! But who?

A thought kept coming into my mind, but I kept pushing it back. 'I've waited a long time for this!' she had said. That meant it was someone old, and probably someone sick.

At last, the thought broke free in my head, and as I ran along the road I cried out, 'Grandfather!'

A Chat in the Night

It's not a good idea to run too fast at night, even when the moon is up, and I was soon reminded of that. As I tore into our yard, my foot clipped a stone and I was sent flying headlong through the air. I landed on my face in the dirt, and what little wind I had left was knocked out of me.

I lay there, gasping for breath, and as I sucked in air, a smell came in with it. A strong, sweet smell, a warm, comforting smell, the smell of all smells I most wanted to smell at that moment: the smell of Grandfather's pipe.

I raised my head a little, and there in front of my nose were two brown, hobnailed boots. I looked up and saw that the rest of my grandfather was connected to those boots. He was looking down at me with his hands on his hips.

He stooped down, grabbed me by the arms and put me standing on my legs. 'Now then, lad, what's all this about?'

'Grandfather!' I gasped, catching hold of his hand, 'I–I–I thought–'

'Calm down, lad, take it easy. Take a few deep breaths.'

I did, and when I'd recovered a bit, I said, 'Grandfather, I *saw* her!'

'Her?' he repeated. 'And just who might "her" be?'

'*Her*! The Banshee!'

'You *saw* her?' he said, taking the pipe out of his mouth. 'You mean you *heard* her. So did I. Your father was in his workshop using a circular saw, and your mother was inside listening to the radio, so they didn't.'

'But I *saw* her too, Grandfather!' I insisted. 'And – and – and I thought she was coming for *you*.'

Grandfather put his arm around my shoulders. 'Come along into the hayshed,' he said, 'and we'll talk. We can't discuss it in the house because your mother wouldn't like it.'

We traipsed away into the hayshed and sat down on a couple of old boxes. There was a tilly lamp hanging from a rafter, and Grandfather lit it.

It gave off a loud, hissing sound and a bright, yellow light, and it felt safe and sort of cosy in there. We hadn't drawn in our haycrop yet, so Grandfather was able to keep his pipe going.

'Now, Jimmy,' he said, when we were comfortable, 'tell me the whole story. Begin at the beginning.'

When I'd finished, Grandfather sat for a long time, scratching his head and fiddling with his pipe. After a bit, he knocked the dottle out of it and refilled it from his tobacco pouch. He struck a match, and when he had the blue smoke curling up around him, he said, 'Jimmy, when I told you before about old Miss Hegarty, I didn't tell you the full story. Maybe now it's time I did.

'When my old grandfather (may the Lord have mercy on his soul) was a boy, he heard stories from the old people of the village about an old Miss Hegarty, she used to live down where the old ruined house is now. Apparently, she was a strange sort of woman. She lived all alone, and she knew things that other people didn't know in those days: the names of the stars, the properties of herbs and many other things. Now, in those days, people were very superstitious, and because of the way she lived, they thought she was a witch, or that she was in league with the fairies. She never did any harm to anyone – quite the opposite, in fact, because she used to cure sick people and injured animals – but people were afraid of her just the same.

'Anyway, one night, the Banshee was heard in the village, and everyone was looking out to see who was going to die. Only nobody did. But then someone discovered that old Miss Hegarty had disappeared. A big search was mounted, but no trace was found of her.

Nobody knew where she'd gone, but there were two schools of thought: some people thought the Banshee had carried her away, but others believed the Banshee would have no power over her because she had been in league with the fairies all the time, and had gone away with them into the west, to Tír na nÓg – the Land of Eternal Youth. Anyway, no one ever found out the truth of it. That's the story my old grandfather heard, and that was supposed to have happened before he was born.'

Here Grandfather paused and relit his pipe, which had gone out. 'But when my grandfather was about eight years old,' he went on, 'a young woman appeared below around Hegarty's place. Nobody knew where she'd come from, and she didn't make them any the wiser. She said her own name was Hegarty, and she laid claim to the old house. Well, by that time, the roof had fallen in, and as nobody else had any claim to it – or wanted it, for that matter – nobody argued with her.

'She fixed up the old house and settled down and lived away there, all alone. In all the years that followed, she never revealed to anyone where she'd come from. Some people thought she was the old Miss Hegarty's granddaughter, or some other relation. But a few of the older folk remembered the old stories and claimed that she was the same woman, come back from Tír na nÓg after all those years, with her youth restored.'

Grandfather shrugged and spat on the ground. 'Who knows?' he said. 'Stranger things could happen.

'Anyway, things went along so, and the years passed. And, strangely enough, this woman was able to work cures, just like the first Miss Hegarty, and she did a lot of good around the neighbourhood and was well thought of. Well, it happened one day that my grandfather had a sick sheep, and he went down to Hegarty's to see if the woman – she was old by this time – could do anything for him. But when he got there, the house was empty. He didn't take any notice of that, because she often used to go away gathering herbs and so on, but when she didn't app-ear after a few days, people began to worry. A search was started, and this time the police were called in. The whole countryside was scoured for her, but not a sign of her was ever seen again.

'Everyone knew the old story about how the first Miss Hegarty had disappeared, and this seemed just too much of a coincidence! More and more people be-gan to believe that the rumours about Miss Hegarty and the fairies and Tír na nÓg were true, and they avoided the place. They thought it was haunted.

'After a time, the old people died away, one by one, and the old story died with them, and people began to go down there again to visit the old wishing-well. Nothing was ever heard of Miss Hegarty. But, judging by what you've just told me, it looks as though she's back again!'

I had listened in silence to every word Grandfather had said. It was such an amazing story! A couple of big moths were flying wildly around the lamp, and the old man got up to adjust the flame. As he did so, I said, 'But what about the Banshee, Grandfather? Where does she come in?'

He looked down at me, with his pipe between his teeth. 'The Banshee is a different kettle of fish entirely, Jimmy. I heard her last night, and again tonight, and you heard *and* saw her. Someone's for the high jump, depend upon it!'

He sat down again on the box and put another match to his pipe. 'I'm the oldest man in the village,' he said, 'so it could well be me she's after, especially since I haven't been feeling too spoony lately!'

'Don't say that, Grandfather!' I cried. But he only gave a grim little laugh.

'Don't worry about it, Jimmy, I'm not bothered. I've been around a good while, and I'm not afraid to go. But I'm a tough old bird, and if it's me she's after, she won't have any great parcel going, I'm nothing special!'

He said something more after that, about wanting to use up the last of his tobacco before she got him, but I wasn't listening. It had all fallen into place for me. The Banshee's words came back to me: 'This one is special! I've waited a long time for this!' And Miss Hegarty had said: 'Now it's time you were going. I'm expecting another visitor tonight.'

I knew who the Banshee was after now, and it wasn't Grandfather. It was Miss Hegarty!

(15)

A Reckoning

I went into the house and straight up to my room. I threw off my clothes and got into bed, but for all the good it did me I might just as well have been lying on top of a furze bush – I'd have had just as much chance of falling asleep. My mind was going around in circles, and I couldn't shake off this awful feeling that something bad was going to happen to Miss Hegarty and it was all my fault. If I hadn't made my wish, she wouldn't have got involved in the first place. That isn't to say I was sorry for the wish, because I wasn't, and I would have wished it again if I had to, but I still felt sort of responsible.

I lay there, trying to think of something I could do. Maybe, I thought, if I went and made another wish, the Banshee would go back to wherever she came from. But Miss Hegarty had told me you only get one wish, and I had used mine. I tried to put it all out of my mind and fall asleep, but I just couldn't.

I was still mulling it all over when I heard a sharp tap at the window. I held my breath and strained my ears – like when you think you hear a mouse in your room, but you aren't sure – and a second later there came another, louder tap. Someone was throwing pebbles at the glass.

I got up, went across to the window, opened it and looked out. Who do you think was standing there? None other than Julia McGrory.

When she saw me looking out, she said in a sort of loud whisper, 'Come down!'

'What d'you mean?' I asked. 'What d'you want?'

'Come down and I'll tell you!' she hissed.

'Go away!' I said. 'It's after midnight. What are you up to?'

She hopped from one foot to the other, as if the ground was hot under her feet. 'Please come down,' she repeated. 'It's important!'

Her voice was getting louder, and the last thing I wanted was for her to wake up everyone. So I said, 'All right, but keep quiet! I'm coming.'

What else could I do? I mean, if they found her under my window in the middle of the night, I'd never hear the end of it.

I slipped into my clothes and tiptoed down the stairs, out the back door and around to where Julia was waiting.

'What's going on?' I demanded. 'What're you doing here? You should be home in bed. There's people trying to sleep and–'

'Stop talking and listen!' she snapped, cutting me short. 'Why d'you always talk so much?' Hearing her say that was the biggest surprise yet!

'*Me?*' I gasped. '*You're* the one who's always–'

'Will you be *quiet*!' she interrupted again, 'and let me explain!'

With that, she caught me by the elbow and started leading me out towards the road. I shook myself free. 'Where d'you think we're going?'

'Come *on*!' she said impatiently, grabbing my arm again. 'I'll explain as we go.'

'I'm not going anywhere,' I said, digging my heels in. 'Not till you tell me what it's all about.'

She stamped her foot angrily at that. The moon was shining on her face and her eyes were blazing. 'It's Mikey,' she said.

'What about him?'

'I was in bed, asleep, when something woke

me. I think it was a cry of some kind, but I don't know. By the time I was fully awake, everything was quiet. Then I heard Mikey getting up and going downstairs, so of course I got up too, to see what he was about. I followed him downstairs and spoke to him, but he didn't answer, it was like he was sleep-walking. He walked out to the road, and I went back in to get my shoes and coat. By the time I came out again, he'd gone away down the road as far as the footbridge – I could see him standing on it in the moonlight. And...and then.' She passed her hand over her hair and hesitated.

'Then *what*?'

'Then someone came onto the bridge and spoke to him. It was weird!'

'Who?' I said, feeling a sort of prickle at the back of my neck. 'Who spoke to him?'

'I–I can't be sure, but I think it was that woman.'

'You mean–'

'I mean that woman we met on the bridge – the scary one. I hurried down to the bridge, but when I got there, there was no one, only Mikey walking away on the other side. I ran after him and tried to talk to him, but he just kept on walking and wouldn't say anything. It was like he was in a trance. I was scared, and I wanted to go home and wake my mother and father, but I was afraid I'd lose sight of him and no one would know where he'd gone, so I stayed with him. But he kept walking faster and faster, and in the end I couldn't keep up. When I came around the bend of the road here, I'd lost sight of him, so I came down here. I don't know where he's gone!'

I knew. There was only one place. And without thinking, I blurted it out, 'Hegarty's well!'

'Hegarty's well?' repeated Julia. 'Why would he go there at this time of night?'

'There's no time to explain,' I said, grabbing her by the hand. 'Come on!'

We ran out to the road and off towards Hegarty's place. I must have been sort of pulling Julia, because after a bit she gasped out, 'Will – you – let – me – go! I can run just as well without you dragging me!'

I let her go, and we carried on. By the time we came to Hegarty's laneway, we were both out of breath. Julia kept saying, 'Tell me what's going on!' and, 'Why are we here?'

At the bottom of the laneway, we stopped. 'Listen, Julia,' I said, 'this might be dangerous. Maybe you'd better stay here.'

At that, she started trembling, and in the moonlight I could see tears in her eyes, but she bit her lip and said, 'I'm frightened, Jimmy, but if it's dangerous for you – and Mikey – then I'm coming.'

Well. You couldn't help but admire her, could you? I mean, it's easy to be brave when you're not afraid, but when you're scared and still don't back away, that shows real courage, doesn't it? To tell the truth, I was pretty frightened myself – in fact, I was shaking in my shoes, but if Julia could be brave, I decided, I could too. I grabbed her hand and we tiptoed into the yard. It was as silent as a tomb, and there was no sign of Mikey or you-know-who.

As quietly as we could, we stole along the side of the old ruin and peeped around the corner. And what we saw made my eyes bulge out and my throat go dry. And for once in her life, Julia didn't have anything to say either.

Mikey was kneeling down in front of the well, his hair standing up in spikes like a hedgehog. And alongside him, her arms folded, the red-haired woman was standing, smiling her horrible, cake-eating smile as she stared at him.

'Tha-a-a-t's-s i-i-i-t!' she hissed. 'You've done it before. Now reach in and pick out Jimmy's three-penny bit. Be careful,' she added, 'don't splash. I don't care for that water.'

I sucked in my breath and pulled my head back. Julia ducked back too. 'What is it, Jimmy?' she whispered. 'What's going on? What did she mean?'

'I can't tell you,' I croaked, 'there isn't time. All I know – at least, I think I know – is that if Mikey takes that coin out of the well, Katie McCafferty will–' I stopped and shook my head. I'd already said too much. I knew what I had to do, but I didn't know if I had the courage to do it!

'Stay here, Julia,' I said, and, taking three deep breaths, I jumped around the corner.

Mikey was lying down on the flat stone, his hand in the water. 'No!' I shouted. 'Stop!' I sprang forward, grabbed his ankles and yanked him backwards. His face bumped off the ground a few times, but with a face like Mikey's that didn't really matter.

But the next second, it wasn't Mikey's face that was worrying me, but my own neck. With a fearful shriek, the Banshee leapt at me and caught me by the throat. She lifted me clear off the ground, so that my feet were dangling in the air, and brought my face right up against hers. I was so close to her I could see little veins running through the whites of her red-rimmed eyes. She was hissing like a snake.

'You've called the tune once too often, *Mr Well-wisher*!' she said through her teeth. 'Now it's time to pay the piper!'

The blood was singing in my ears by now, and things were beginning to go black in front of me when a low voice coming from behind me said, 'Let him go. It's me you want.'

The Banshee looked over my shoulder, and straightaway that horrible, cake-eating smile appeared across her face. And the next thing I knew, I was sailing through the air. I landed on my backbone – or, to be more exact, the part lower down. I sat there, shaking my head, until I was able to see properly again.

To my left, Mikey was getting to his feet, and Julia was helping him, and in front of me, with her hands at her sides, Miss Hegarty was standing face-to-face with the evil, sneering, red-haired woman.

'At last!' the Banshee crowed. 'I knew you'd show yourself! Twice before, you cheated me – and death – by escaping to Tír na nÓg. Two hundred years and more I've waited, but now you're mine!' She stretched her arms out wide, and her red eyes blazed with the most fearsome light, and even though there was no breeze, her long hair swirled and waved around her head.

'Wait!' said Miss Hegarty.

She stooped down and scooped up a palmful of water from the well, then turned to Mikey and Julia. Wetting her thumb, she traced the sign of the well on each of their foreheads.

'Take them home, Jimmy,' she said, turning to me. 'They will remember nothing of all this; they must not, since their wishes are still unfulfilled. Go now. Don't look back.'

And with one last flash of her beautiful smile, she turned once more to face the Banshee.

I got to my feet, and, grabbing hold of Julia, who had hold of Mikey's hand, I made for the laneway as fast as I could.

When we arrived out at the road, Julia looked around and said, 'What are we doing here?'

Mikey stared at her and then at me. He rubbed his hand over his face. 'What are these bumps on my face?' he asked.

'Come on,' I answered. 'We have to get home. I'll explain later.'

We parted company outside my house, and as I turned for home I could hear them arguing as they hurried off towards their house.

'But what time is it?' Julia was saying. 'And why aren't we at home in bed?'

16

A Sign in the Sky

I got up extra early the next morning, and before school I hurried off down to Hegarty's place again. In the bright sunshine it seemed like a different place, and when I got to the bottom of the little laneway, I realised that it *was* different.

Something terrible had happened there during the night. Branches had been torn off the trees, and in places whole bushes had been uprooted. It was as if a hurricane had swept through the yard or some great battle had taken place between giants. Even the old house hadn't escaped unscathed: parts of the walls that had been standing the night before had been flung down, and stones were scattered around everywhere.

But, astonishing as all that was, there was a bigger surprise in store for me. I walked around to the back of the house, and who was standing there by the well only Katie McCafferty!

She spun around when she heard my footsteps, and we both blurted out together, 'What are you doing here?' And then, of course, we started laughing.

'You go first,' I said.

'I had to come,' she said. 'I spent the whole night dreaming that I was here – by the well. And there were two women here, and for some reason they were fighting over me!'

'What happened?' I asked faintly.

Katie pulled a face. 'I don't know why,' she said with a frown, 'but it's getting hard to remember. It was all clear in my mind this morning. Isn't that strange? But I remember that one of them was trying to take me away, and the other was trying to stop her. The one that was trying to take me pulled me up the laneway, but then the other one pulled her back down here, and I got free. I started running then – at least, I think I did – and then...then I woke up! Wasn't it strange?'

I nodded, but said nothing. We stood there together for a long time, just looking down into the well.

After a while, Katie said, 'We'd better go, Jimmy. We'll be late for school, and it's my first day back. It won't do to upset Mr O'Shea!'

We turned away and began walking across the yard, but before we'd gone very far, Katie stopped. 'I nearly forgot!' she said with a chuckle, and ran back to the well. She took a coin out of her pocket and flipped it into the water, closing her eyes and crossing her fingers.

'I wonder if they ever come true?' she said as she ran back to me.

'You never know,' I said. 'Maybe some do and some don't.'

We made our way back towards the laneway. As we did, I glanced back. I wished I knew what had happened to Miss Hegarty, and I was half-hoping that there would be some sign there to tell me, but there wasn't.

But just as we reached the top of the lane, Katie pointed at the sky and said, 'Look, Jimmy! Isn't that strange?'

I looked up. High overhead a flock of wild geese was winging its way out over the coast into the west. It was very strange to see wild geese at all at that time of year, but what was stranger still was the formation of the flock. It looked like this:

ALSO BY DAN KISSANE

JIMMY'S LEPRECHAUN TRAP

Surely leprechauns are cute little fellows who do no harm to anyone? *Be warned!* They are nasty little creatures, just waiting for the chance to trick someone and gain power over them.

When Jimmy meets up with one of them, very strange things start to happen. But how can he get rid of him? Maybe Grandfather has the answer. Can they trap this clever little fellow and outwit him?

Paperback €5.95/stg£4.50/$7.95

PUGNAX AND THE PRINCESS

Desperate to be wise, the King of Wisdom wants to get the Book of Riddles, but it is in the grimy hands of Prince Pugnax of Porzana. The King arranges for his daughter, Princess Ricolana, to marry the dreadful prince. She is heart-broken – but what can she do? Along comes Agamemnon who, with a little help from a strange wizard, sets out to rescue – and maybe win – the princess. But nasty Pugnax is not a man to take this kind of challenge lying down ...

Paperback €6.50/stg£4.99/$5.95

THE EAGLE TREE

Prince Pugnax of Porzana is not a happy man. In fact, as a result of a disagreement with a wizard, he's now a giant cockroach! The Prince was horrible as a human, so the people of Porzana are glad to be rid of him.

Then Pugnax is declared officially dead and his nephew, Bembex of Bellonia, is to inherit Porzana. This greedy villain plans to cut down all of Porzana's forests for paper. There's only one thing to be done – Bring Back Pugnax! And for this all hope depends on the heroine Freddie Fennifeather, the strange Black Donald and the wizard McCracken.

Paperback €5.07/STG£3.99/$7.95

Send for our full-colour catalogue
